Snoopy and the Magical Sneakers

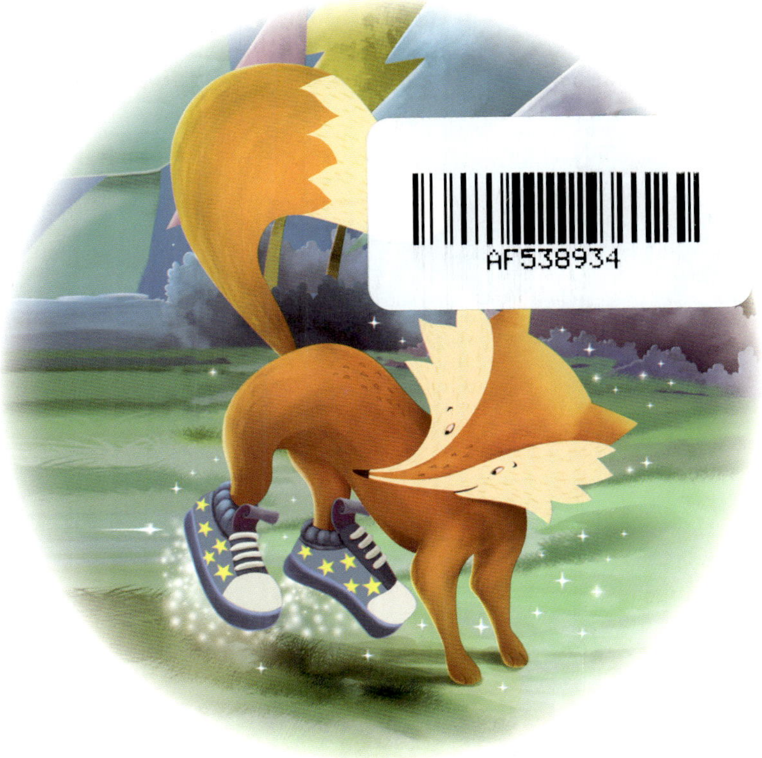

An imprint of Om Books International

Reprinted in 2025

Corporate & Editorial Office
A-12, Sector 64, Noida 201 301
Uttar Pradesh, India
Phone: +91 120 477 4100
Email: editorial@ombooks.com
Website: www.ombooksinternational.com

Sales Office
107, Ansari Road, Darya Ganj
New Delhi 110 002, India
Phone: +91 11 4000 9000
Email: sales@ombooks.com
Website: www.ombooks.com

ISBN: 978-93-85273-88-9

Printed in India

10 9 8 7 6 5 4

Snoopy and the Magical Sneakers

I'm all set to read

Paste your photograph here

My name is

____

Snoopy was a **sneaky** fox. He was called **Snoopy** because he liked to **snoop**. Every night, whether it rained or **snowed,** **Snoopy** went **sniffing** in the forest and **snatched** anything he found.

One night, when **Snoopy** was **sniffing** around, he saw two funny looking things. He went closer and stuck his **snout** into one of them. They turned out to be a pair of **snazzy sneakers**! He decided to **sneak** off with them at once.

Snoopy's paws were cold, so he wore the **sneakers**. They were a **snug** fit. Suddenly, **Snoopy** got lifted right off the ground. The **sneakers** were magic flying **sneakers**.

Snoopy was floating in the air! Higher and higher **Snoopy** rose, till he was flying over the trees.

Soon, the magic **sneakers** were taking **Snoopy** to different places. He soared over forests and sparkling rivers.

Finally, the **sneakers** brought **Snoopy** down to an empty farm. Suddenly, there was a loud noise. "Rrrroooooaaaarrrrrr!!! Ppphееееwwwwww!!!" This scared **Snoopy**, so he hid behind a drum. It was a huge dog, **snoring** in its sleep!

Snoopy stepped on a twig as he tried to **sneak** away. **Snap**! The **snoring** dog **snorted** and woke up. He **snarled** at **Snoopy**. But **Snoopy** didn't have to worry. The **sneakers** had already zoomed off with him.

This time, **Snoopy** landed near a large moving rock. He heard a loud **sneeze**. **Snoopy** went around the rock to find out who was there. To his surprise, he saw that the rock was actually a giant **snail** with a bad cold.

"Who are you?" the **snail snapped** at **Snoopy**. **Snoopy** told the **snail** that he was lost. "I have a friend who will help you," said the **snail**, **sniffling**. His cold was really bad.

Before **Snoopy** could find out more, the **sneakers** had taken off with him again. **Snoopy** wondered where they were going next. Soon, **Snoopy** was soaring over a desert. He could hear a faint **snip-snip** sound.

"The **sneakers** have brought me to the **snail's** friend!" said **Snoopy** hopefully. He followed the **snip-snip** sound till he met a **snake**.

It was a **rattlesnake**. **Snoopy** pleaded the **snake** to send him home. The **snake** looked **snootily** at **Snoopy** at first. But then, he agreed.

The **snake** started making the **snip-snip** sound again. And as he did, **Snoopy** rose higher in the air. The **sneakers** zoomed at top speed as they soared across the **snow**-capped mountains. Finally, **Snoopy** reached the forest where he had found the **sneakers**.

A wizard in a deep blue cloak was watching **Snoopy** angrily. "So you are the thief that stole my magic **sneakers,**" said the wizard, **sneering** at poor **Snoopy**. "Shall I trap you in my hat or turn you into a **snivelling** rat?" he **snapped**.

Snoopy shook with fear. He took off the **sneakers** and gave them back to the wizard. He promised never to **snatch** or steal again. He just wanted to go home and **snuggle** into his bed.

The wizard was kind. He let **Snoopy** go. **Snoopy** thanked the wizard and returned home. He had a nice **snack**. Soon, he was **snoozing** and dreaming of the magic **sneakers**.

Know your phonic words

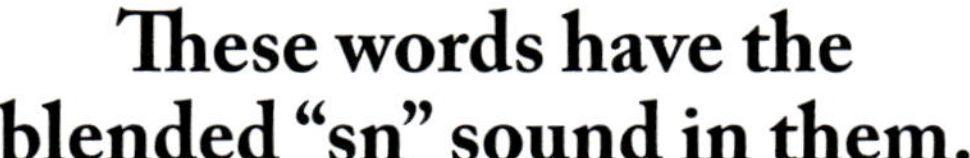

These words have the blended "sn" sound in them.

Snoopy
sneaky
snoop
snowed
sniffing
snatched
snout
snazzy
sneakers
sneak

snug
snoring
snap
snorted
snarled
sneeze
snail
sniffling
snip-snip
rattlesnake

snootily
sneering
snapped
snivelling
snuggle
snack
snoozing
snow

Know your words

Snoop – to watch without being seen

Sneakers – (Usually) shoes with laces

Snug – comfortable

Snazzy – stylish

Snivel – to cry and sniffle